BEAST QUEST

FERNO THE FIRE DRAGON

Adam Blade

First published in Great Britain in
2007 by Orchard Books Ltd
This Large Print edition published
by BBC Audiobooks
by arrangement with
Orchard Books Ltd 2008

ISBN: 978 1405 662420

Series created byWorking Partners
Ltd, London
Text copyright ©Working Partners
Ltd 2007
Cover illustrations ©
David Wyatt 2007
Inside illustrations ©
Orchard Books 2007, courtesy of
Orchard Books Ltd

British Library Cataloguing in Publication Data available

Printed and bound in Great Britain by
Antony Rowe Ltd., Chippenham, Wiltshire

With special thanks to
Stephen Cole

For Jamie Morgan

Welcome to the kingdom of Avantia. I am Aduro—a good wizard residing in the palace of King Hugo. You join us at a difficult time. Let me explain . . .

It is written in the Ancient Scripts that our peaceful kingdom shall one day be plunged into peril.

Now that time has come.

Under the evil spell of Malvel the Dark Wizard, six Beasts—fire dragon, sea serpent, mountain giant, horse-man, snow monster and flame bird—run wild and destroy the land they once protected.

Avantia is in great danger.

The Ancient Scripts also predict an unlikely hero. It is written that a boy shall take up the Quest to free the Beasts from the curse and save the kingdom.

We do not know who this boy is, only that his time has come . . .

1

We pray our young hero will have the courage and the heart to take up the Quest. Will you join us as we wait and watch?

Avantia salutes you,

Aduro

PROLOGUE

Caldor the Brave stood at the foot of the mountain. His bronze armour gleamed in the pale morning sunlight.

'The fire dragon is close. I can feel it.' The knight pointed his sword up towards the mist at the top of the mountain. 'For the sake of our kingdom, it must be stopped!'

'Good luck, sir,' said Edward, his page.

Caldor held out an armoured hand and placed it on Edward's shoulder. They both understood that they might never see each other again.

The knight turned to climb the smooth, dark slope. His feet slipped and skidded on the rock. But he dragged himself up with determination, slowly climbing higher and higher. Soon the mist closed behind him and he was lost from sight.

All that was left was an eerie silence. Edward shivered.

Suddenly the mountain started to shake.

Edward could feel the vibrations travelling through his feet and up his legs. He stumbled and his chin hit the ground as a huge judder threw him to the ground. There was a metallic taste in his mouth. Blood!

What was happening?

'Caldor!' Edward yelled, scrabbling to his feet as the rocks shifted beneath him. 'Come back!'

But his voice was lost in the grinding sounds that filled the air. The whole mountain shook violently. Was it about to come crashing down on him?

Edward was seized with panic. Heart pounding, he looked up and saw two overhanging rocks start to move. Their razor-sharp edges glinted in the sunlight as they edged out. Suddenly, they slashed through the air like giant axe-heads. Edward flinched.

As the mist cleared, he glimpsed Caldor clinging to the side of the mountain. Then something reared up beyond the knight, and Edward saw the flash of an eye and the thick scales of leathery skin. It was the spiked head of a huge dragon!

Suddenly everything made horrible sense. His master had been right. The Beast was close. This wasn't a mountain . . . it was the dragon itself! Glancing down with a rush of fear, Edward realised that he was standing on the dragon's tail—and that Caldor was holding onto the monster's back! And those two overhanging rocks were the dragon's mighty wings. He wanted to run, but his legs were frozen with fear.

Now he could see the sides of the dragon moving in and out as it breathed heavily. Steam hissed out of the creature's nostrils.

'Caldor, come back!' Edward yelled again. But a terrifying roar drowned out his words.

The dragon's wings unfolded again, stretching out to beat the air in a deadly rhythm.

'It's taking off!' Edward shouted. 'Caldor, quick—'

'Get back!' Caldor's words carried faintly on the air. 'Go to the city. Warn King Hugo. Run!'

Before Edward could move, the dragon flicked its tail, sending him flying. He hit the ground hard, shaking and gasping for breath, as the terrifying Beast rose up into the air. Caldor's screams filled his head.

Edward struggled to his feet and tried to run after his master, but the dragon was already high above him. It let out a huge roar, and a jet of orange flame lit up the sky. As it disappeared into the distance, one of Caldor's gauntlets, scorched and smoking, clattered to the ground beside Edward. Clutched in its fingers was a golden key.

The echoes of Caldor's cries hung in

the air. Then, silence. The knight was gone.

And his mission to free the fire dragon from Malvel's curse had failed.

CHAPTER ONE

THE MYSTERIOUS FIRE

Tom stared hard at his enemy. 'Surrender, villain!' he cried. 'Surrender, or taste my blade!'

He gave the sack of hay a firm blow with the poker. 'That's you taken care of,' he announced. 'One day I'll be the finest swordsman in all Avantia. Even better than my father, Taladon the Swift!'

Tom felt the ache in his heart that always came when he thought about his father. The uncle and aunt who had brought Tom up since he was a baby never spoke about him or why he had left Tom to their care after Tom's mother had died.

He shoved the poker back into his pack. 'One day I'll know the truth,' he swore.

As Tom walked back to the village, a sharp smell caught at the back of his throat.

'Smoke!' he thought.

He stopped and looked around. Through the trees to his left, he could hear a faint crackling as a wave of warm air hit him.

Fire!

Tom pushed his way through the trees and burst into a field. The golden wheat had been burned to black stubble and a veil of smoke hung in the air. Tom stared in horror. How had this happened?

He looked up and blinked. For a second he thought he saw a dark shape moving towards the hills in the distance. But then the sky was empty again.

An angry voice called out. 'Who's there?'

Through the smoke, Tom saw a figure stamping round the edge of the field.

'Did you come through the woods?' the man demanded. 'Did you see who did this?'

Tom shook his head. 'I didn't see a soul!'

'There's evil at work here,' said the farmer, his eyes flashing. 'Go and tell your uncle what's happened. Our village of Errinel is cursed—and maybe all of us with it!'

Tom turned and ran as fast as he could, stumbling over the blackened tree roots.

Tom burst into the village square, gasping for breath. It was full of villagers. What were they all doing here? It wasn't market day. They were shouting and waving their hands at his uncle, who was standing on a bench at

13

the edge of the square.

'Fire in the fields! What next?' one man shouted.

'The troubles get worse each day!' called another villager.

'The Beasts have turned evil!'

Tom knew that Avantia was said to be protected by six Beasts, including a fire dragon, but no one was sure if they really existed.

'Have you seen the river?' a woman asked. 'It's so low we will soon run out of drinking water.'

'We're cursed,' an old man wailed.

'I don't believe in curses,' said Tom's uncle firmly. 'But our village needs help. One of us must go to the king and request his aid.'

Tom stepped forward. '*I'll* go to the palace.'

The villagers laughed. 'Send a boy on such a mission? Ha!'

'The king would laugh at us for sending a child.'

Tom's uncle spoke quietly. 'No, Tom. You're too young. I'm head of the village. I'll go.'

Suddenly a small boy, smeared in soot, pushed through the crowd. 'Help!' he gasped. 'Please help! Our barn is on fire!'

'Men! Bring your pails to the river now!' Tom's uncle roared to the crowd. 'The rest of you bring spades to the barn—if we can't quench the fire we'll bury it. Quickly!'

Tom looked at his uncle as the men rushed to obey. 'The village needs you here as its leader, Uncle Henry,' he said. 'Please let me go instead.'

Tom's uncle turned to face him, his

face serious. 'I suppose I have to let you out into the world sooner or later,' he said. He stared into the distance. 'Perhaps it's meant to be . . .' He shook himself and turned back to Tom. 'Yes, you must go to the king. And there is no time to waste—you will have to leave first thing tomorrow!'

CHAPTER TWO

JOURNEY TO THE CITY

It was dark when Tom began his journey. But as the sun rose, he saw that Errinel wasn't the only place in trouble. As he strode further away from the village, he passed countless fields that had been scorched black. Dry ditches traced paths where streams had once flowed.

He kept walking through the morning and into the afternoon, ignoring his tired muscles and aching feet. As he drew nearer the city, other people joined him on the dusty road. Horsemen cantered past and donkeys weighed down with packs trudged along steadily, driven on by families walking beside them. He could hear people muttering to each other. They seemed to be fleeing famine and danger. Clearly, he wasn't the only one heading to the palace to ask for help. Tom started to walk faster.

The towering city gates stood before him at last. They were wide open. As he passed through them, Tom felt a new surge of energy. He was here at last! He pushed his way through the narrow, crowded streets. He had one aim—and that was to get to the palace as quickly as possible. He could see it up ahead. It dwarfed all the other buildings with its purple spires and domes of sea-green glass. Tom had never seen anything like it!

But as he stepped through the main gateway into the palace courtyard he groaned. In front of him was a long line of people, and it was barely moving.

'Here to see the king's clerk?' a soldier asked Tom.

'No, I'm here to see the king!' Tom told him.

The soldier laughed. 'You'll have to see the king's clerk first. It's up to him who sees the king. Stand in line. You've a long wait.'

'I can't wait here!' Tom said. 'My village needs help—fast!'

'All of us need help,' retorted a stout man with a beard that reached down to his knees. 'In the West we've been hit by tidal waves. We need to build sea-barriers, but we can't do it without help from the king!'

'There are terrible blizzards in the North,' said an old woman. 'The whole kingdom is in danger! And mark my words—the Beasts have done this.'

'The Beasts?' scoffed the stout man. 'You must be joking!'

The woman glared at him angrily. 'If no one believes in the Beasts, how will they ever be stopped? Something has happened to turn them against us. Yes, something evil has disturbed the Beasts . . .'

'What do you mean?' Tom asked.

But the woman turned her back on him and walked away.

Tom found himself thinking of the dark shape he had glimpsed amongst the hills back in Errinel. Could that have been a Beast? Could it have been the fire dragon? Tom looked at the long line of people in front of him again and made up his mind. He'd come to ask the king for help—and that was exactly what he was going to do—even if it meant breaking into the palace. 'While there's blood in my veins,' he swore, 'I'm going to save my village!' He pushed his way back through the crowds and out of the palace courtyard.

When night had fallen, Tom started to circle the palace walls. Pale moonlight shone down upon him. 'What I need is an open window,' he muttered under his breath. 'Or an unlocked door.'

But guards were posted all the way round the palace. Tom crept towards the eastern gateway, but it was manned by two burly men in brown uniforms.

Suddenly there was the sound of running footsteps behind Tom. A ragged lad stumbled out of the dark night.

'Open the gates!' the boy shouted hoarsely. He was around Tom's age, and was covered in dirt. In one hand he clutched a blackened gauntlet and in the other a parchment scroll. 'I bring word from Sir Caldor. I must see the king!'

The guards opened the gates, leaving them ajar, and ran to help the boy.

'This is my chance!' Tom thought.

CHAPTER THREE

THE KING'S COURT

Tom sprinted through the gateway while the guards' backs were turned, and hid in the shadows by the wall, edging his way round the courtyard. The smell of roasting meat wafted across from an open door. His stomach growled loudly.

'The palace kitchens must be in there,' he said to himself. 'If I go in, maybe I'll find a way of getting to the king.'

As soon as Tom walked through the door, he was struck by heat so fierce it reminded him of his uncle's forge back in Errinel. Huge iron cauldrons hung over open fires. Kitchen maids milled about, stirring the stew or laying out food on silver platters.

A large woman bustled up to him. 'Ah, at last!' she cried. 'You must be the new kitchen boy.'

'What? Oh yes, that's right,' Tom agreed quickly.

'I'm Cook,' the woman continued. 'Thank goodness you're here! I've got two serving girls off sick and the king's supper is almost ready. You can take him what little food we have left.'

Tom couldn't believe the palace was short of food. The kingdom's troubles were even worse than he had imagined.

Tom followed Cook to where platters of food waited, ready for serving. A steward gave Tom a quick lesson in balancing a platter on one hand held high above his head. Then he led Tom and the other servants up to the royal dining chamber.

Tom's heart beat fast. There, seated at a long table lit by tall candles, was King Hugo. He looked younger than Tom had imagined, with thick dark hair and large brown eyes. He wore velvet green robes and was surrounded by grim-faced lords and ladies. Squaring his shoulders, Tom carried his platter to the far end of the table.

'I have to talk to the king,' he told himself. 'Errinel is relying on me.'

Next to the king sat a short, elderly man with a wispy beard. He was dressed in a gown of faded blue and red silk, with a pointed hat perched on his head. The old man's grey eyes seemed to glow in the candlelight, as brightly as the jewel he wore on a chain around his neck.

'Isn't it only wizards who dress like that?' Tom thought.

'Well, messengers would look pretty stupid in these clothes, wouldn't they?' said the old man with a smile.

Tom gasped. 'You read my mind!'

'That's because I *am* a wizard. Wizard Aduro,' the old man murmured, looking closely at Tom.

'But what are *you*, I wonder . . . ?'

Just then the dining chamber doors flew open. The ragged young boy Tom had seen at the gates scrambled inside. Two guards followed closely behind him.

'Forgive me, sire,' the boy cried. He sank to his knees before the king and held out the scorched gauntlet. Tom noticed that a golden key was clutched in its fingers. 'I am Edward, page to Caldor the Brave. My master is dead.'

'Dead!' echoed the king, jumping to his feet. He leaned forward, his knuckles turning white as he gripped the edge of the table. 'It cannot be!'

'It is true, sire.' The boy's eyes brimmed with tears. 'He's been burned to death by the fire dragon, Ferno. Our Quest is over.'

Tom could hardly believe his ears. So the Beasts *were* real!

King Hugo turned to stare out of a window carved into the thick walls of the castle. Through the window, Tom could see the city stretching far out into the night, its lights twinkling. 'My bravest knight has perished,' the king cried in despair. 'Avantia is doomed!'

Wizard Aduro walked to the centre of the room. His face was grave, but he seemed calm. 'The king's council has urgent matters to discuss,' he announced. 'I must ask all servants to leave us at once.'

Escorted by two guards, the serving staff left the dining room, murmuring as they went.

'I'm not going!' Tom thought. This was his chance to find out exactly what was going on.

'Hurry up there!' the guards ordered, pushing past Tom as the last stragglers left the room.

Thinking quickly, Tom doubled back to hide behind a large pillar near the king's chair. He pressed his cheek against the cold stone. His heart was thumping so loudly that he was sure someone would hear it.

'Curse the Dark Wizard Malvel!' cried one lord. 'We *must* break this evil spell he has placed upon the Beasts, before the fire dragon, Ferno, destroys us all!'

An evil spell! Tom gasped loudly, then slapped a hand over his mouth.

Edward the page whipped around. 'Who's that in the shadows?'

'A spy!' exclaimed King Hugo.

'Please, let me explain!' Tom begged as two guards lunged towards him. He dodged out of the way, but a third threw himself at Tom's legs. Tom leapt over him and cried out to the king, 'I'm only here because I want to save lives!' The guards grabbed him by the arms.

'Enough!' thundered Wizard Aduro, and everybody froze.

'Take him to the dungeons,' ordered King Hugo, walking towards Tom. He gazed down at him.

Tom had never looked into the eyes of a king before. He bowed his head.

'Away!' King Hugo called, waving a hand towards the doors. 'Take him away.'

Just then Aduro appeared at the king's side. 'This boy is here for a good reason. I can feel it.'

The guards stopped in their tracks.

'Are you sure?' King Hugo asked after a long pause.

Aduro pointed at Tom. 'Can't you see the likeness?' he asked.

King Hugo peered at Tom, then shook his head.

Tom blinked. The likeness? What was Aduro talking about?

Once again the wizard seemed to read his mind. 'I'll show you,' he said, his eyes meeting Tom's.

As Tom watched, a small, flickering flame appeared in the palm of Aduro's upturned hand. Tom gasped as the flame turned violet.

King Hugo looked at Tom through the magical fire, and his eyes widened. 'It cannot be! But . . . it is. This is the son of Taladon the Swift!'

CHAPTER FOUR

A QUEST

'Taladon!' Tom echoed in shock. 'You knew my father, Your Majesty?'

'Oh yes,' the king said, smiling. 'One of the bravest men I have ever known.'

A link with his father at last! Tom felt tears pricking his eyes. The king had seen what Tom had never been able to picture. His father's face.

'Do you know where he is now?' Tom asked, hoping he wasn't being disrespectful.

King Hugo and Aduro exchanged glances. The lords and ladies of the king's council were all listening intently, leaning forward over the dining tables.

The king waved a hand through the air. 'It was a long time ago that I knew him . . .' he said, lifting Tom's chin to get a better look at him. 'What is your name, boy?' he asked.

'Tom,' the wizard answered for him. 'Your Majesty, I must speak with you and Tom alone.'

King Hugo nodded to the members of the council. 'You may go. Please treat Edward the page as your honoured guest.'

Edward bowed and joined the lords and ladies as they left the room.

As the doors closed, the wizard took the king to one side. Tom strained to catch their conversation as they talked in heated whispers.

At last, King Hugo beckoned to Tom. He approached nervously. What was the king going to say? Was he going to send him away?

'Tom, our land is in terrible danger,'

said the king. 'The Dark Wizard Malvel has hunted down the ancient Beasts and somehow he has gained power over them all.

'The six Beasts have watched over Avantia and protected us from danger since the first settlers arrived,' continued King Hugo, pacing the room. 'Ferno the fire dragon keeps southern Avantia safe. He makes sure the water supply never dries up. The other Beasts each have their duties, too. But now they have turned against us and carry out terrible acts of destruction in Malvel's name. Even my bravest knights cannot tame them.'

'Who is Malvel?' asked Tom.

'Once he was a good man, with a good life,' said King Hugo. 'But his happiness did not last. He fell victim to that dreadful disease—envy.'

Aduro took up the story. 'He was jealous of the Master of the Beasts and his special connection with our kingdom's most powerful creatures. So he searched out forbidden knowledge – wisdom and power dating back to the Dawn of the Beasts.'

Tom's mouth felt dry. 'And Malvel found that knowledge?'

'Yes. The power that he gained then made him evil, and gave him the strength to break the magical bond between the Master and his Beasts. Ever since, the Master has been imprisoned and Malvel controls the Beasts.'

'What do we need to do?' Tom asked.

'Malvel's magic is powerful,' Aduro said. 'Our only hope is that we can find someone with the power to free the Beasts one at a time, and return them to goodness so that they can continue to protect our kingdom rather than ruin it. But,' he warned, 'we mustn't let our people know the Beasts really exist. These creatures can only do their work if they're left in peace. That's why we've always pretended that the Beasts are not real.'

'Malvel has made the Beasts almost unstoppable,' the king continued. 'Ferno is burning all our crops and blocking up the rivers. And the other Beasts—a sea serpent, a mountain giant, a horse-man, a snow monster and a flame bird—are causing floods, avalanches and chaos elsewhere. They will destroy Avantia unless we set them free from Malvel's wicked enchantment. That is why I sent Sir Caldor to try to unlock the collar that Malvel used to charm the dragon.' He handed Tom a large golden key. 'Only this will undo the lock.'

Tom slowly turned the key over in the palm of his hand. It was very big, but weighed nothing. He realised it was the key that he'd seen held in Caldor's scorched gauntlet. He looked back up at the king, a question in his eyes.

'The key was created by Aduro,' the king murmured, 'but must be put to use by a hero. Your father once served me—now I ask you to do the same. Aduro's magic has shown me the strength and honour within you. I'm sure you are a match for any knight in my kingdom.' He smiled. 'Fate sent you here, Tom. Now I wish to send you on a secret mission…'

A shiver of excitement ran down Tom's spine.

The king leaned forward. 'Will you risk your life for the Beast Quest?'

'I will,' Tom said without hesitation. He had never been more sure of anything in his life. 'Whatever it takes— I *will*!'

CHAPTER FIVE

GATHERING STORM

Tom woke early the next morning.
Where was he? As he looked round at
the big stone windows and the painting
on the wall he suddenly remembered.
He was in the king's palace, in one of
the royal guest bedrooms! Excited, he
jumped out of bed immediately.

New clothes and a silver chainmail
vest had been laid out on a wooden
chest near the door. Tom slipped on
the dark trousers and woollen, long-

sleeved top. Then, with a thrill of delight, he tried the chainmail on for size. It was beautifully made and a perfect fit. Over that he wore a plain brown tabard to hide the armour. After all, his Quest was a secret one.

Tom smiled proudly as he looked at his reflection in the mirror. He looked ready for his adventure. Then he felt a moment of doubt.

'Can I really succeed where Avantia's bravest knights have failed?' he wondered.

'Yes, you can,' came a soft voice behind him.

With a start, Tom turned to find Aduro at the door. He was holding a sword and a large wooden shield.

'You may think you are an unlikely hero,' Aduro went on. 'But in these strange times, all things are possible.'

Tom nodded. 'I suppose they are.'

Aduro stepped into the room. Slowly, Tom knelt on the cold stone floor before him. He didn't know why, but it felt like the right thing to do. Aduro raised the sword into the air and for a moment Tom could swear that it glowed, lighting

46

up the dust that danced through the air around him.

Aduro and Tom gazed up at the sword, then Aduro brought it down so that the tip of the sword rested gently on Tom's chest, next to his heart. 'May this boy have the strength of heart to save Avantia.' The wizard's voice rang round the room. Tom bent his head. Then Aduro drew the sword away and gently pulled Tom to his feet. Smiling, Aduro held the hilt of the sword out to Tom. 'For you,' he said, simply.

Tom took the sword. It fitted his grip perfectly, and felt far lighter than the poker he was used to. 'Perfect,' he said.

Now Aduro passed him the polished wooden shield. It was well-crafted, but very plain. Tom remembered seeing knights occasionally riding through his village with their bright, colourful shields. He couldn't help feeling a twinge of disappointment.

'Appearances can be deceptive,' Aduro smiled, again reading Tom's thoughts. 'On your Quest you will find allies in the strangest of places, and in the unlikeliest of forms. But you have a wise head, Tom. Trust your instincts. Now, I have other gifts for you.' He took a parchment scroll from his pocket. It was just like the one Edward the page had been holding the night before.

As Aduro unrolled it, Tom saw it was a map of Avantia. He stepped forward to get a better look and, as he watched, the map came to life! Trees and hills and mountains rose up from the paper, standing as tall as Tom's thumb.

Cautiously, he reached out to touch one of the white mountains in the north. His finger came away glittering with frost.

Tom looked up at Aduro, startled. The wizard nodded at the map.

'Look closer,' he commanded.

Now Tom saw tiny, twisting paths spring up like veins on the pale parchment. They slowly spread across the map towards the south-west where a mountain stood, dark and unwelcoming.

'Ferno's mountain,' guessed Tom.

'Yes.' Aduro held up the golden key Tom had been shown the night before. A loop of leather cord had been threaded through it, and Aduro hung the key around Tom's neck like a medal. 'Only if you set Ferno free can we begin to put right Malvel's evil. You must unlock the enchanted collar that imprisons him.'

'I will do all I can,' Tom promised.

'Now, you must go,' Aduro said, handing Tom the map. 'Your horse is waiting for you outside.'

Tom took his sword and shield and

followed Aduro through the palace and out to the stable yard, where a groom stood with a jet-black stallion. At the sight of Aduro, the horse whinnied in greeting and tossed his head. It had a white mark in the shape of an arrowhead between its eyes, and the brown leather of its saddle gleamed brightly.

'The stallion's name is Storm,' said Aduro. 'He is young and fast.'

Storm pulled away from the groom and trotted over to them. He pushed his nose against Tom's shoulder and gazed at him.

Tom beamed. 'I think we'll get along well, Storm,' he said.

Aduro held his sword and shield as Tom scrambled up onto the horse's back, then handed them up to him.

Tom looked down at the wizard. 'What will happen to my village, and my uncle and aunt? They are relying on me to help.'

'A cart is on its way there with food and water,' said Aduro. 'The driver will tell your uncle that you have been sent on a special errand for the king—

and that you will return when you can.'

Tom patted Storm's neck. 'Thank you, Aduro—and goodbye!'

'Farewell, my young friend. All our hopes go with you.'

Tom nodded and kicked his heels against Storm's sides.

Storm cantered away, out through the palace courtyard and into the hectic city streets, his hooves clattering on the cobbles as he swerved round carts and passers-by. Tom saw the open city gates looming up ahead, and felt his face flush with excitement. Soon he would be on his own. 'Faster, Storm!' he urged.

Storm galloped out through the gates, and, as they burst onto the grassy plains outside the city, Tom gave a wild whoop. This was it! His adventure had begun!

Not only was Storm the fastest horse Tom had ever ridden but he also seemed to understand exactly what

Tom wanted him to do. He slowed down at the slightest pull on the reins and sped up the second Tom touched his sides with his heels.

By late afternoon they had reached the southern edge of the grassy plains. A vast forest stretched out before them. It looked dark and mysterious and rather forbidding, but the map

showed that the quickest way to the dragon's mountain was to cut straight through the forest.

'Come on, Storm,' Tom said, carefully guiding the stallion into the trees. 'I think it's this way.'

The trail twisted and turned. As they headed deeper into the forest, the trees seemed to get thicker and press

closer. Far above him, the sky was dull, and Tom felt a wave of panic as the gnarled trees and bushes seemed to be reaching out to grab him. Storm's ears flicked as if he sensed Tom's concern.

They carried on until they came to a small clearing, where the path seemed to end. Tom dismounted. Pulling his sword from its sheath, he started slashing at the dense undergrowth to clear a way forward.

A rustling sound caught his ear. He stood still and listened.

'Who's there?' Tom called.

There was no answer.

Pressing on, Tom chopped through a thick tangle of brambles. His heart filled with dread. This place didn't feel right, and now he was sure that something awful was watching him. But taking hold of Storm's reins, he began pushing his way through the thicket.

Graagh! A set of gleaming, yellow fangs snapped in his face.

With a shout of alarm, Tom leapt back against Storm. A wolf!

Its grey and white fur was matted,
and its amber eyes were wild and
staring. Its huge paws were like clubs,
and ended in lethal claws. Its teeth
were bared in a vicious growl as it
prepared to spring!

CHAPTER SIX

THE FOREST OF FEAR

Storm reared up, kicking out with his
front hooves, and Tom threw himself
into the brambles and bushes. But the
wolf didn't attack them. It was
growling at something else. Something
that was crashing through the
undergrowth towards them.

Suddenly, three soldiers smashed
their way into view. Their eyes flashed
fiercely through the slits in their
helmets. One held a crossbow while

the other two waved long swords. The wolf advanced towards them, its growl growing angrier.

'We'll teach that brat and this vermin to steal from our king!' snarled the first soldier, aiming his crossbow at the wolf's head.

'No!' Tom scrambled up from his hiding place—just as the soldier fired an arrow. Without thinking, Tom threw his sword. It spun through the air and sliced the short, heavy arrow in half before plunging into a tree trunk.

'Another poacher! Get him!' One of the soldiers charged at Tom with his sword raised. But the wolf threw itself at the man's legs, knocking them from underneath him. Outraged, the other two soldiers charged towards Tom.

Tom grabbed Storm's reins and swung himself up into the saddle. Leaning down low, he rushed at the men with the wolf growling at his side, sending them running. Pulling Storm back round, he wrenched his sword from the tree trunk and rode towards the soldiers once again, scattering them into the woods. The wolf pulled

ahead, darting through the trees onto a narrow path. Tom and Storm galloped after him.

The wolf moved like the wind, only slowing once it had led Tom and Storm a safe distance from the soldiers. Tom eased Storm down to a trot.

Then the wolf stopped, and suddenly, right in front of it, a figure dropped from the trees onto the path. It was a girl.

She was tall and skinny, dressed in breeches and a dirty shirt. Her black hair was short and messy, and her face was red with scratches. In one hand she clutched a bow, and in the other a quiver of arrows. As she crouched to greet her wolf, she looked at Tom, her green eyes narrowing.

'It's all right, I'm not trying to hurt him,' he promised as Storm stopped. 'My name's Tom,' he said, dismounting. 'We weren't chasing him —he was leading us away from the soldiers.'

The wolf padded over to him, and pushed his nose into Tom's hand.

The girl relaxed and smiled at him warmly. 'Well, Silver seems to like you and he's a good judge of character. If he trusts you, then so will I.'

'How did you get him?' Tom asked, as Silver bounded back to the girl and sat down at her feet, looking adoringly up at her.

'I found him injured on a hunting trip,' the girl replied. 'I nursed him till he was well again, and we've been friends ever since.' She stepped forward, took Tom's hand and shook it firmly. 'My name's Elenna.'

'What are you doing in the middle of the forest?' Tom asked.

Elenna frowned. 'My uncle's a fisherman. Silver and I wanted to try our luck on the river. But it's dried up and now we're far from home, with

nothing to fish for and nothing to eat.'
She sighed. 'So we came to the forest
to hunt rabbits. But the soldiers
thought we were after the king's deer.
They chased after us and we got
separated.'

There was a sudden crash and more
shouting behind them. Storm reared
and Silver's hackles rose.

'Quick! We'd better get out of here!'
said Tom. 'They're still coming after
us!'

Putting his foot in a stirrup, he swung
himself onto Storm's back. Seeing
Elenna hesitate, he grabbed her hand
and helped her scramble onto the
stallion behind him.

Storm leapt forward into a gallop.
They raced through the forest, Elenna
clinging to Tom, Silver darting
alongside them.

To his relief, the soldiers were no
match for Storm's swift hooves. Soon
their shouts died away in the distance.
Tom drew Storm back to a walk. 'I
think we're safe,' he said, as they
reached a small clearing.

Elenna slid down from Storm's back

and looked up at Tom. 'What's going on?' she asked. 'You're wearing chainmail—I could feel it. But you're too young to be a knight.'

Tom hesitated. Something told him he could rely on this girl, and Aduro had told him to trust his feelings. He knew his task was to be kept secret, but perhaps he *could* tell Elenna about his Beast Quest.

'It's the Beasts,' he began. 'I've been chosen to release them from an evil wizard's spell.'

'You?' said Elenna. 'But you're just a boy!' She looked hard at Tom. He stared back undaunted. 'But I can see why they've chosen you . . .' she added. Then she raised her eyebrows. 'I've always thought the Beasts were more than just a story . . .'

'They are,' Tom told her.

She looked at him, wide-eyed and eager. 'So tell me about them.'

'They've been turned evil. Ferno the fire dragon is under a spell—'

'Ferno?' she gasped.

'He's burning all the crops. And the river's dried up. If I can't stop him,

Avantia will be plunged into famine.'

'I knew nothing natural could make an entire river dry up overnight . . .' Elenna muttered. She bit her lip, then nodded as if she had reached a decision. 'I can't let you do this on your own. I'm going to come with you.'

Tom grinned. He'd be glad to have a friend by his side as he faced the fire dragon. But then he remembered what had happened to Caldor. 'You can't,' he said. 'It's far too dangerous!'

'Not as dangerous as you doing it all by yourself!' Elenna shot back. She took a step closer. 'You saved us from the soldiers. We owe you. Besides . . .' She hesitated. 'There's something special about you. I'd like to help. I can help. I know my way around this part of the kingdom. Let me—please.'

Tom looked into Elenna's eyes. He knew she meant every word. 'What about your family?' he asked.

Elenna shrugged. 'My parents died in a fire years ago. My uncle and his family look after me now.'

'I live with my aunt and uncle, too!' Tom interrupted.

Elenna smiled thinly. 'I don't know what your uncle's like, but I don't think mine would notice if I disappeared for a bit.'

Tom felt a stab of pity and realised how lucky he was. He thought about Errinel, his safe house and his warm bed. Then he pushed the thought out of his mind. He needed to stay strong for the Quest.

'Well,' said Elenna. 'Can I come?'

'Yes!' Tom said. 'I'll be glad of the company.'

Elenna let out a whoop of delight. Silver jumped round her legs, barking excitedly.

'So, where do we find this dragon?' she asked, as she calmed the wolf.

Tom patted his pocket. 'I have a map to show me,' he said quietly. 'The big question is—what do we do once we find him?'

CHAPTER SEVEN

DAWN OF THE DRAGON

Tom, Elenna, Silver and Storm cleared the forest at the end of the first day and were now travelling across rocky ground. They had been travelling without rest for two days and two nights. Desperately tired, they'd camped out last night. They'd all slept heavily, apart from Silver, who had kept an ear out for danger. But morning had soon come, and the fire that had warmed them through the night was dying now. Tom opened the map and studied it.

'Let me look!' cried Elenna, running to kneel next to Tom. Ever since he had first shown her the magical map, Elenna had been fascinated by it.

'We're very close to Ferno's mountain now,' he said. 'I reckon the Winding River should be near here. But I haven't seen anything.'

Elenna pointed through the mist to a massive stack of boulders piled up across the valley below them. 'Perhaps the river has been dammed up by all those rocks.'

Tom pressed his finger against the river on the map, and, sure enough, it came away bone dry. 'I think you're right,' he said. 'Come on. It's light enough to get moving now.'

The sun rose slowly and the mist began to clear. They looked out across the land, at the slope of distant rocky hills and the jagged shapes of far-off mountains. Tom felt a tingle start in his chest and creep through his body. Somewhere out there, his destiny was waiting—and so was Ferno the fire dragon.

Later that day they reached the rocky hills. They began to climb and, after a while, arrived at a plateau. The mist was thicker here.

Then suddenly Storm threw back his head and whinnied, and Silver's hackles rose in warning.

'What's got into them?' asked Elenna nervously.

'I don't know.' Tom drew his sword and unhooked his shield from his back. Then he walked on alone a little way.

Suddenly, through the mist, a dark shape loomed ahead of him. Tom clutched his sword more firmly as he felt a shiver of anticipation.

But the shape didn't move. Steeling himself, Tom walked a little closer. 'It looks like a steep rocky slope,' he said. 'Slate, I think.'

'The animals don't like it,' called Elenna.

The key in Tom's pocket began to feel warm. Was it reacting to something close to them, or was he imagining it? 'I'm going to explore,' he said, looking back at Elenna. 'There's something here.'

Elenna lifted her bow and pulled out an arrow from her quiver. 'I'm coming with you,' she said firmly. Tom knew it would be hopeless to argue with her. 'Don't even think about leaving me behind,' she said, testing the point of the arrow with her thumb.

'I wouldn't dare,' Tom smiled, glad she was with him. Then he looked back at the rocky slope, his smile fading. It was time.

Leaving the animals where they were, Tom and Elenna started walking up the slope. The slate was black and glassy, like no rock Tom had seen before. Then he felt a faint vibration under his feet.

'Hold still,' he told Elenna. 'Something's happening.'

They listened, but no—nothing. Only the vibration, pulsing through the rock beneath their feet.

Pulsing like a heartbeat.

Tom crouched to take a closer look at the slates. They seemed to shine like dark scales.

Scales?

'Back!' Tom shouted. 'Get back to the animals, to the real hill.'

Elenna stared at him. 'What do you mean, the real hill?'

'This isn't slate,' Tom cried, grabbing hold of her hand and pulling her along after him. *'It's dragon skin!'*

Suddenly a terrifying roar rang out around them. Beneath their feet, the ground shifted. They threw themselves off the slope and down to the plateau where Storm and Silver had been pacing anxiously. Silver howled, while Storm skittered backwards.

Tom had never been so frightened in all his life.

'What are we going to do?' Elenna shouted. 'Shall we run?'

Clutching his shield tightly, Tom tried to think. He was on a Quest for the king—he couldn't run away now.

But before Tom could reply, the Beast began to rise from the rocky surface, up and up . . .

Ferno the fire dragon was gigantic. Towering over them all, with his huge, jagged wings extended, he blocked out the sky. His head was coal-black and spiky; and tight around his neck was the enchanted collar, held in place by a golden lock that glowed with a strange, magical light.

Tom gasped. So this was what a Beast looked like! Ferno was as big as a mountain. What chance did a boy

have against such a brute?

But as he looked at Elenna standing beside him, bravely clutching her bow and arrow, and as he thought of his friends and family back in Errinel, he knew that however slim his chances, they were worth taking.

'While there's blood in my veins,' he vowed, 'and for the king and my father, I'll see this through.' Just saying the words immediately made him feel braver.

Tom stared up at the dragon as it swung its huge head to and fro above them. 'We *must* get that collar off,' he said. 'That's what is controlling him and making him evil. If we can do that, Ferno will go back to protecting the kingdom instead of destroying it.'

Elenna clutched hold of Silver for comfort. 'But how will we ever *reach* the collar?' she asked.

Slowly the dragon lowered his head, sniffing the air, his eyes bright and blood-red. His dreadful gaze fell on them. Tom stared deep into the Beast's eyes, mesmerised, and saw himself reflected back in the huge pupils.

Ferno was so close Tom could feel the heat of the dragon's breath on his face. The seconds pulsed by slowly, then Tom snapped out of his trance. With a gulp, he brandished his sword and stood his ground.

Ferno reacted quickly. Uncoiling his huge forked tail, the dragon lashed it out like a deadly whip. But before it could knock Elenna and Tom off their feet, Silver bravely pounced. He snapped his teeth into the scaly flesh at the thin tip of

Ferno's tail. With a roar, Ferno jerked his tail up into the air with Silver still clinging on. The dragon's tail went whistling over Tom and Elenna's heads, whipping Silver through the air. Flung like a catapulted stone, the wolf landed with a thump on the rocky ground and lay still.

'Silver!' cried Elenna, sprinting towards him.

'No, Elenna!' Tom shouted. 'Keep still! Stay there!'

But Ferno had noticed Elenna's sudden movement. He opened his massive jaw, letting out a furious roar. Then he pulled back his head and prepared to strike.

'He's going to attack Elenna!' Tom realised in horror. 'She won't stand a chance!'

CHAPTER EIGHT

FINAL COMBAT

Tom swung round and whistled to Storm. The jet-black stallion galloped up to him. 'Come on, boy,' Tom cried, leaping into the saddle. 'We've got to save Elenna!'

Tom touched his heels to Storm's sides, and the horse leapt bravely forward. Over the pounding of the stallion's hooves, Tom could hear another roar building in the dragon's throat.

'Elenna, look out!' Tom shouted.

Elenna looked round and saw the dragon's huge, open mouth above her. She froze.

As Storm galloped past Elenna and Silver, Tom hurled himself from the horse's back. He landed badly and pain shot through his ankle, but there was no time to stop. There was a boulder on the hillside close by. If they could all just get behind it . . .

But it was too late.

Ferno's eyes narrowed to fierce slits. With a roar, he blasted an enormous fireball from his mouth. Ignoring the pain in his ankle, Tom threw himself in front of Elenna and held up his shield. The fireball hit the wooden shield with such force that Tom staggered back. Flames hissed angrily round the edges of the shield, singeing the hairs on Tom's arms as he struggled to hold it between them and the fireball. The heat burned Tom's throat as he gulped the air, and he could see Elenna's eyes watering, leaving tracks in the dirt on her face. But the shield that Aduro had given him held out—they were safe! The dragon retreated, throwing a final, frustrated hiss over his shoulder. But Tom knew Ferno would return…

Frantically, he threw the shield on the ground to smother the flames, and soon only thick black smoke remained in the air. The shield was scorched, but it was still in one piece. Tom swung it

over his shoulder, strapped it into place and helped Elenna up. He could feel her trembling. 'Are you all right?'

Elenna nodded her head slowly, her eyes wide in shock. 'I think so, thanks to you and Storm. But what about Silver?' The wolf was still lying unconscious on the ground.

'We can't help him until we've dealt with Ferno,' Tom told her gently. 'If that Beast roasts us, nobody will be left to look after Silver.'

'You're right,' Elenna said. 'But how?'

Tom whistled for Storm. Neighing loudly, the horse trotted up through the curtain of smoke.

'Well done, boy, you were very fast,' Tom told him. 'But now you've got to be even faster.' He scrambled up into the saddle. Then he leaned down and passed his sword to Elenna. 'Protect yourself with this.'

'What are you going to do?' she asked.

'I'm going to free the dragon!' Tom cried, unfastening his shield and hooking his arm through it, ready for battle. 'Wish me luck!' With a whoop, he dug his heels once more into Storm's sides.

The horse shot like an arrow in the direction the dragon had taken.

A few moments later, out of the smoke and mist, Ferno reared up ahead. Hearing Tom and Storm, he turned his huge head towards them. Spreading his wings, he pulled back to strike.

It was now or never. Fighting to keep his balance, and wincing at the pain in his ankle, Tom moved into a crouching position in the saddle. The horse raced towards the Beast's outstretched right wing. At the final moment Storm ducked to gallop beneath it, and Tom leapt into the air. With a thump, he landed on top of Ferno's wing. It felt hard as stone, but blood-warm. The dragon flapped his mighty wings in slow, jerky sweeps. Struggling to find a handhold, Tom felt himself start to slip.

With a furious hiss, the dragon whipped round and thrust his head up close to look at Tom.

Seizing his chance, Tom dipped under the Beast's craggy chin and threw himself at the enchanted collar around its neck.

'Got you!' he cried, slipping his left arm through over the golden edge of the collar. Under here he was safe from the dragon's fire—but now Ferno was throwing his head from side to side, trying to shake him off.

Tom felt as though his arm was about to be torn off, but he gritted his teeth and held on. With his free hand he pulled the key from around his neck and tried to fit it in the lock. But the constant movement of the dragon made it impossible. He tried to steady himself and managed to get the tip of the magic key to the edge of the lock.

)!

ed in anger. The noise was Tom's arm burned with the world started spinning . Then, as the dragon flung up, the key slipped from gers and fell to the ground far below.

'No!' Tom yelled.

85

The dragon threw his head forward and twisted his neck, but still Tom clung on. He had been so near. So near to victory. But now what could he do to get the key back?

Suddenly, through the drifting smoke, he saw Elenna below, climbing onto Storm. She was holding her bow and arrow, and it looked as if she meant to use it. But she was aiming the arrow at *him*!

'Your shield!' she yelled. 'Tom, use your shield!'

'What? What are you doing?' he shouted in confusion. Quickly, he shifted his grip on the collar and raised his scorched shield—just as Elenna released the arrow.

With a *thunk* it landed in the scorched wood. Tom peered over the top of the shield.

There was the key. Elenna had found it and tied it to the end of the arrow. Good old Elenna! Tom pulled the arrow and the key out of the shield.

The dragon lunged forward and breathed another deadly fireball at Elenna, but Storm was quicker. He thundered over the scorched grass, carrying her clear of danger. The dragon shook his head in fury.

Tom felt his strength return. With the key in his hand, there was still hope!

For an instant the dragon was quiet. Quickly, Tom pushed the key into the lock. It turned with a smooth click.

The enchanted collar glowed a brilliant blue for a moment, then it faded away to nothing.

'I did it!' Tom thought. 'I really did it!'

Then, in the same split-second, he realised that now, with the collar gone, he had nothing to cling on to but the key. With a shout, Tom found himself plunging towards the ground . . .

But as Tom fell, the key suddenly rose in the air above him, pulling his arm up. Somehow, it was slowing his fall! He felt the wind rise and carry him over to where Elenna and Storm stood waiting. He landed softly beside them.

'Yes!' he shouted, dazed and jubilant. Ferno had been freed—and it felt as though he had set free something in himself, too. All his doubts and fears of failure melted away. The dragon would threaten the kingdom no longer, and Tom—with the help of his friends—had been the one to put things right.

'Tom, you were almost flying!' gasped Elenna. 'How did you do that?'

'It was the key,' he said, holding it up in awe.

Just then Silver bounded through the smoke towards them. He was all right!

Elenna gathered up the panting wolf

in a hug, but her green eyes were still troubled. 'What about Ferno?'

Tom turned to face the Beast. He loomed over them, and Tom had to lean back to see Ferno's red eyes, which were still fixed on him. But this time, Tom wasn't afraid.

'You're free now,' he called out softly. 'Free to protect our land and people.'

The fire dragon shook out his powerful wings. He dipped his huge head at Tom to acknowledge him and then he took flight.

Tom and Elenna watched in silence as Ferno swooped over the dry riverbed and lashed out with his tail at the barrier of boulders. The huge rocks shattered and a wave of clear water surged down the riverbed like a caged creature released.

'This was just for starters, Malvel!' Tom shouted, punching the air. 'I won't rest until *all* the Beasts are free!'

Elenna and Tom could see Ferno drinking deeply from the water of the river. Then he threw back his spiky head, roared, and launched himself into the air, leaving a rainbow of fire across the blue sky. The dragon swooped over Tom and Elenna's heads, and flew towards the horizon. They watched as he disappeared into the distance.

Elenna turned to look at Tom. 'How are you feeling?' she asked.

Tom could feel his eyes brimming with happiness. 'Like a hero,' he replied.

Storm neighed and Silver howled as if they both agreed with him. Elenna and Tom burst out laughing.

'Now the only question is—what next?' said Tom.

CHAPTER NINE

THE BEGINNING

'What's that?' Elenna pointed at Tom's pocket.

Something inside was glowing. Light spilled out from Tom's trouser pocket.

Tom quickly reached inside, pulled out the magical map and unrolled it. A puff of silver smoke escaped from the tiny palace marked on the parchment. It rose up before them, growing steadily larger.

Slowly, it started to take shape, and

soon Tom could make out the shadowy outline of a man. Two points of silver light sparkled in the cloud of smoke and grew brighter, twinkling merrily, until Tom realised what he was looking at.

'Aduro!' Tom gasped, recognising the twinkling blue eyes of the good wizard. The rest of Aduro took shape in the smoke.

'Well done, Tom,' said the wizard. 'And you, too, Elenna. Avantia owes you both a great deal.'

'How are you doing this?' Tom asked. 'How can you see us?'

'Remember the jewel I wear around my neck?' The wizard smiled. 'With that I can see over all the kingdom.'

'Then you saw everything that just happened with Ferno?' Elenna asked.

'I did,' said the wizard. 'And I've told King Hugo about your success. The palace is filled with celebration! You both showed great courage and determination. You are true heroes. But are you ready for your next Quest?'

A tingle crept down Tom's spine.

'The other Beasts have to be freed, too,' he said, excited and nervous all at once.

Aduro nodded. 'But first, Tom, there is a gift waiting for you.'

'A gift? Where?' asked Elenna.

Tom shook his head, baffled. Then he noticed something glinting in the scorched branch of a nearby tree. He looked at Aduro, an unspoken question in his eyes. Aduro nodded

95

again, and Tom ran to the tree, climbing up to retrieve whatever was caught there.

It was a reddish black dragon scale, gleaming like jet. 'It's beautiful,' he murmured, dropping back down to the ground. 'What a souvenir!'

'It is much more than that,' said Aduro. 'You have earned it by winning your battle with Ferno. Now, if you place it in your shield, it will deflect all kinds of heat!'

Elenna pointed to a scorched groove at the bottom of the shield. As Tom reached out his hand towards it, the groove opened. Tom pressed the scale into place like a jigsaw piece. There was a bright ruby glow and then the wood closed around the edge of the scale, leaving it glinting like a jewel in the light.

'Now, there is no time to waste,' Aduro said. 'You must follow the path on the map to the next stage of your Beast Quest!'

Tom and Elenna gazed at the map. A snaking green path was starting to form on the parchment, stretching across to the Western Ocean.

'What about our families?' Tom asked. 'Can we send a message to them?'

'I'll make sure your families aren't worried,' the wizard promised. 'But the secrets of your Quest may not be shared with anyone.'

'We understand,' said Elenna.

Tom thought about his uncle and aunt, and about his father, Taladon the Swift. Not *all* of his family knew Tom had left the village of Erinnel. His father didn't know—wherever he was.

'Now I must leave you,' said Aduro. His image began to dissolve like smoke in the breeze. 'Good luck, my young friends.'

'Wait,' said Tom urgently. 'What about my father? Will I ever know what happened to him?'

'You will learn a lot on this Quest, Tom,' said the wizard, his words echoing into the air. 'Farewell . . .'

The image of Aduro faded. All that was left was a sparkle in the air where the wizard's eyes had been.

Tom looked again at the map. The green path led to a tiny image of a sea serpent, rising up and making splashes with its tail.

He felt his blood chill and his mind darken. He pictured himself struggling in foaming black water against a huge, writhing enemy. He could almost feel enormous ivory fangs closing down around his body, and sense fierce eyes staring into his soul.

He shook his head quickly and his doubts cleared.

He swung up onto Storm's back. Aduro was right—there was no time to waste. Another Beast had to be set free from Malvel's curse.

Elenna climbed up behind him and Silver trotted alongside, both eager to get going.

Tom pulled his sword out of its scabbard and raised it up, pointing high in the sky.

'Onwards!' he shouted.

Then, sliding his sword back into its sheath, he dug his heels into Storm's side and the horse leapt forward. Tom and Elenna were on their way to the next Quest. Tom didn't know what was waiting for him.

But he knew he was ready.